TIMELESS CLASSICS

A CHRISTMAS CAROL

Charles Dickens

– ADAPTED BY –

Emily Hutchinson

SADDLEBACK
EDUCATIONAL PUBLISHING

TIMELESS CLASSICS

Literature Set 1 (1719-1844)

A Christmas Carol
The Count of Monte Cristo
Frankenstein
Gulliver's Travels
The Hunchback of Notre Dame
The Last of the Mohicans

Oliver Twist
Pride and Prejudice
Robinson Crusoe
The Swiss Family Robinson
The Three Musketeers

Literature Set 2 (1845-1884)

The Adventures of Huckleberry Finn
The Adventures of Tom Sawyer
Around the World in 80 Days
Great Expectations
Jane Eyre
The Man in the Iron Mask

Moby Dick
The Prince and the Pauper
The Scarlet Letter
A Tale of Two Cities
20,000 Leagues Under the Sea

Literature Set 3 (1886-1908)

The Call of the Wild
Captains Courageous
Dracula
Dr. Jekyll and Mr. Hyde
The Hound of the Baskervilles
The Jungle Book

Kidnapped
The Red Badge of Courage
The Time Machine
Treasure Island
The War of the Worlds
White Fang

SADDLEBACK
EDUCATIONAL PUBLISHING
www.sdlback.com

ISBN-13: 978-1-61651-073-2
ISBN-10: 1-61651-073-0
eBook: 978-1-60291-807-8

Printed in the United States of America
15 14 13 12 11 1 2 3 4 5

| Contents |

| 1 |

Scrooge's Office

Marley was dead, to begin with. There is no doubt whatever about that. Old Marley was as dead as a doornail.

Of course Scrooge knew he was dead. How could it be otherwise? Scrooge and he were partners for I don't know how many years. Scrooge was his only friend and his only mourner. And even Scrooge was not so dreadfully cut up by the sad event.

The mention of Marley's funeral brings me back to the point I started from. There is *no doubt* that Marley was dead. This must be distinctly understood—or nothing wonderful can come of the story I am about to tell you.

Scrooge had never painted out Marley's name on the sign. Years afterward it still hung above the door: *Scrooge and Marley.* Sometimes people called Scrooge "Scrooge," and sometimes

"Marley." He answered to both names. It was all the same to him.

Scrooge was a very tightfisted man! He was secret, and self-contained, and solitary as an oyster. The cold within him froze his old features and nipped his pointed nose. It shriveled his cheeks and stiffened his walk. It made his eyes red and his thin lips blue. The hair on his head, eyebrows, and chin was frosty white. He seemed to carry his own low temperature with him. He iced his coffee in the summer, and didn't thaw it one degree at Christmas.

Outside heat and cold had little influence on Scrooge. No sun could warm him; no winter weather could chill him. No wind that blew was more bitter than he. No falling snow was colder. No pelting rain was less open to mercy. The heaviest rain, snow, hail, and sleet had only one advantage over him. They often "came down" handsomely—but Scrooge never did.

Nobody ever stopped him in the street to say, "My dear Scrooge, how are you? When will you come to see me?" No beggars asked him for anything. No children asked him what time it was. No man or woman ever asked him directions. Even the blind men's dogs seemed to know him. When they saw him coming, they would tug their owners into doorways. Then they would wag their tails as if to say, "No eye at all is better than an evil eye, master!"

But what did Scrooge care! This was the very thing he liked.

One Christmas Eve, old Scrooge was busy in his counting house. It was cold, dark, biting weather. He could hear the people outside, stamping their feet upon the pavement stones to warm them. The city clocks said it was 3:00 P.M., but it was quite dark already. It had not been light all day. Candles were flaring in the windows of the nearby offices. The fog came pouring in at every chink and keyhole. It was so dense outside that, even though the street was very narrow, the houses on the other side were hard to see.

The door of Scrooge's office was open so he could keep an eye on his clerk. In a dismal little cell beyond, the clerk was copying letters. Scrooge had a small fire in his own fireplace.

The clerk's tiny fire was so much smaller that it looked like one coal. But he couldn't add to it, for Scrooge kept the coal box in his own room. The clerk had put on his white comforter and tried to warm himself at the candle. Not being a man of a strong imagination, he failed.

"A merry Christmas, Uncle! God save you!" cried a cheerful voice. It was Scrooge's nephew, who had just come in.

"Bah!" said Scrooge. "Humbug!"

Fred, Scrooge's nephew, was all in a glow from walking in the fog and frost. His face was ruddy and handsome. His eyes sparkled.

"Christmas a humbug, Uncle?" said the nephew. "You don't mean that, I am sure!"

"I *do*," said Scrooge. "Merry Christmas? Why be so merry? You're poor enough."

"Come, then," laughed the nephew. "Why be so dismal? You're rich enough."

Scrooge had no better answer than to say, "Bah!" again and then "Humbug!"

"Don't be cross, Uncle!"

"What else can I be," returned the uncle, "when I live in such a world of fools? Merry

Christmas! What's Christmas to you but a time for paying bills without money? You find yourself a year older, but not an hour richer. If I had my way, every idiot who goes about with 'Merry Christmas' on his lips would be boiled with his own pudding. Then he ought to be buried with a stake of holly through his heart!"

"Uncle!" pleaded the nephew.

"Fred! Keep Christmas in your own way. Let me keep it in mine."

"But you *don't* keep it."

"Allow me to leave it alone, then," said Scrooge. "Much good it may do *you*!"

"I have gotten some good from many things by which I have not made money," said the nephew. "Christmas is one of those. It is always a good time—a kind, forgiving, pleasant time. It is the only time I know that men and women seem to open their hearts freely. Maybe it has never put any gold or silver in my pocket. But Christmas has always done me good, and *will* do me good. So I say, God bless it! Please don't be so glum, Uncle. Come! Dine with us tomorrow."

"Yes, you have a wife now, don't you?" Scrooge asked in a grumpy voice. "Why did you get married?"

"Because I fell in love."

"Because you fell in love!" growled Scrooge. He spoke as if that were the only thing in the world more ridiculous than a merry Christmas.

"You never visited before I got married. Why use it as a reason for not coming now?"

"Good afternoon," said Scrooge.

"I am sorry, with all my heart, that you won't join us. But I have come in honor of

Christmas—and I'll keep my Christmas humor to the last. A Merry Christmas to you, Uncle!"

"Good afternoon!" barked Scrooge.

At that, his nephew left the room. He stopped to say Merry Christmas to the clerk. Cold as he was, the clerk was warmer than Scrooge, for he said Merry Christmas back.

"There's another one," muttered Scrooge to himself. "My clerk, with 15 shillings a week, and a large family. Even *he* is talking about a merry Christmas. They're all crazy!"

| 2 |

The Day Gets Colder

After Scrooge's nephew left, two other men came in. They now stood, with their hats off, in Scrooge's office. They had books and papers in their hands, and bowed to him.

"Scrooge and Marley's, I believe," said one of the gentlemen, looking at his list. "Tell me, sir—am I addressing Mr. Scrooge or Mr. Marley?"

"Mr. Marley has been dead these seven years," Scrooge said. "He died seven years ago this very night."

"Ah, well, Mr. Scrooge, then," said the gentleman, taking up a pen. "It is good to help the poor. They suffer greatly in this festive season. Many cannot meet their needs. Hundreds of thousands do not have common comforts, sir."

"Are there no prisons?" asked Scrooge.

"Plenty of prisons," said the gentleman, his eyebrows raised in surprise.

"And the workhouses? I trust they are still open?"

"They're very busy," said the gentleman. "I wish I could say they were not."

"Oh! From what you said at first, I was afraid that something had happened to close them," snapped Scrooge. "I'm glad to hear they're still open."

"Well, they do not supply Christmas cheer of mind or body to the poor," returned the gentleman. "That is why a few of us are trying to raise money. We want to buy the poor some meat and drink, and means of warmth. Christmas is a time, of all others, when Want is keenly felt, and Plenty rejoices. What shall I put you down for?"

"Nothing!" Scrooge replied.

"You wish to be anonymous?"

"I wish to be left alone," said Scrooge. "Since you ask me what I wish, gentlemen, that is my answer. I don't make merry myself at Christmas, and I can't afford to make idle people merry. I help to support the prisons and workhouses—they cost enough. Those who are hungry and cold can go there."

"But sir—many *can't* go there. And many would rather die!"

"If they would rather die," said Scrooge, "they had better do it! It would decrease the surplus population. Besides, it's none of my business. It's quite enough for a man to understand his own business and not to interfere with other people's. Mine occupies me constantly. Good afternoon, gentlemen!"

Seeing that it would be useless to argue, the gentlemen left. Scrooge got back to work. He now had an improved opinion of himself and was in a better mood than usual.

Meanwhile, the fog thickened. The ancient church tower became invisible. Striking the hours and quarter-hours in the clouds, its bell vibrated afterward as if its teeth were chattering in its frozen head. The cold became intense. In the main street, men working on the gas pipes had lighted a great fire. A party of ragged men and boys had gathered around it to warm their hands. In bright shop windows, holly sprigs and berries crackled in the fire's heat.

The whole town was getting ready for

Christmas. The Lord Mayor gave orders to his 50 cooks and butlers to keep Christmas as a Lord Mayor's household should. Even the little tailor stirred up tomorrow's pudding in his attic room, while his lean wife and the baby went out to buy the beef.

It got foggier yet, and colder. Yet cold as it was, one boy stooped down at Scrooge's keyhole to sing a Christmas carol. At the first note, Scrooge seized a ruler and struck the door. The young singer fled in terror, leaving the keyhole to the fog and frost.

At last the hour of shutting up the counting house arrived. With ill will, Scrooge got off his stool and nodded to his clerk. Right away, the clerk snuffed out his candle and put on his hat.

"You'll want all day tomorrow, I suppose?" barked Scrooge.

"If that's all right, sir."

"It's *not* all right—and it's not fair," said Scrooge. "If I were to pay no wages for the time, you'd feel ill used, wouldn't you?"

The clerk smiled faintly.

"And yet," said Scrooge, "you don't think *me*

ill used, when I pay a day's wages for no work."

The clerk said it was only once a year.

"A poor excuse for picking a man's pocket every 25th of December!" said Scrooge. "But I suppose you must have the whole day. Be here early the next morning."

As the clerk promised that he would, Scrooge walked out with a growl. The office was closed in a twinkling, and the clerk headed home to be with his family.

Scrooge had a lonely dinner at a nearby tavern and read the newspapers. Then he went home to go to bed.

| **3** |

Marley's Ghost

Scrooge lived in a gloomy suite of rooms in an old and dreary building. Nobody lived there but Scrooge. The other rooms had all been rented out as offices.

Now there was nothing unusual about the knocker on the door, except that it was very large. Let any man explain to me, if he can, how this happened: Scrooge, putting his key in the lock of the door, saw in the knocker—not a knocker, but Marley's face.

Marley's face. It was not angry or frightening. It looked at Scrooge as Marley used to look—with ghostly glasses turned up on its ghostly forehead. As Scrooge stared at it, it became a knocker again.

To say that he was not startled would be untrue. But Scrooge put his hand on the key, turned it, and walked in.

He did pause before he shut the door. He *did* look behind it first—as if he half expected to see Marley's pigtail sticking out into the hall. But there was nothing on the back of the door, so he closed it with a bang.

Scrooge climbed the dark stairs without a candle. Darkness is cheap, and Scrooge liked it. But before he closed the door, he walked through his rooms to see that all was as it should be. Nobody under the table, nobody under the sofa. He made a small fire and checked again. Nobody under the bed, nobody in the closet.

Quite satisfied, he closed the door and locked himself in. Thus safe against surprise, Scrooge took off his tie. Then he put on his robe, slippers, and nightcap and sat down before the fire.

It was a very low fire indeed. Scrooge had to sit close to it before he could feel any warmth. Suddenly, he heard a clanking noise, deep down below. It sounded as if someone were dragging a heavy chain along the floor of the rooms below.

The noise became louder and then seemed to come up the stairs—straight toward his rooms! Scrooge's color changed when the noise came through the heavy door and passed before his eyes. As it stopped at the hearth, the fire leaped up, as if to say, *"Marley's Ghost!"*

The same face, the very same! Marley in his pigtail, and his usual vest, tights, and boots. The chain he drew behind him was long—winding about him like a tail. It was made of cash boxes, keys, padlocks, ledgers, deeds, and heavy steel purses. Yet Marley's own body was transparent. Looking through his partner's vest, Scrooge could see the two back buttons on his coat.

Cold as ever, Scrooge said, "What do you want with me?"

"Much!" It was Marley's own voice!

"Who are you?"

"Ask me who I *was*."

"Who *were* you, then?" said Scrooge.

"In life I was your partner, Jacob Marley."

"Why are you here?"

"It is required of every man that the spirit within him should walk among his fellow men. If that spirit does not do so in life, it must do so after death. It is doomed to wander through the world. It must witness what it cannot share now, but might have shared while on earth!" The Ghost raised a frightful cry and shook its chain.

"You are chained. Tell me why."

"I wear the chain I forged in life," replied the Ghost. "I made it link by link, and yard by yard. I made it of my own free will, and of my own free will I wore it. Is the pattern of this chain strange to *you*?"

Scrooge shrank back in his chair.

"Do you know the weight and length of the heavy chain you bear *yourself*? Seven Christmas Eves ago, it was as heavy and as long as this. You have worked on it since. Yes, yours is a heavy chain!"

"Tell me more. Comfort me, Jacob!"

"I have no comfort to give," the Ghost said. "In life, my spirit never went beyond our counting house. Now I cannot linger anywhere. Weary journeys lie before me!"

"You must be very slow, Jacob."

"Slow!" the Ghost repeated.

"Seven years, and traveling all the time!"

"The whole time," cried the Ghost in a dismal

voice. "No rest, no peace!"

"But you were always a good man of business, Jacob," said Scrooge.

"Business?" cried the Ghost. "Humankind was my business. The common good was my business. Charity, mercy, and kindness were all my business. My trade was but a drop of water in the ocean of my business. At this time of the year, I suffer most. Why did I walk through crowds of fellow beings with my eyes turned down? Why only you can see me now, I do not know. I have sat invisible beside you many and many a day."

It was not a happy thought. Scrooge shivered, and wiped his brow.

"I am here tonight to warn you. You may yet have a chance and hope of escaping my fate. A chance and hope that *I* got for you, Ebenezer."

"You were always a good friend to me," said Scrooge. "Thank you!"

"You will be haunted by Three Spirits. Without their visits, you cannot hope to avoid the path I walk. Expect the first tomorrow, when the clock strikes one. Expect the second on the next night at the same hour. The third will come on the third night. Look to see me no more. Remember what has passed between us!"

With that, the Ghost walked backward from Scrooge. With each step it took, the window raised itself a little. When the Ghost reached it, it was wide open. In a moment, the Ghost floated out into the dark night.

Scrooge closed the window and checked the door. It was locked, as he had locked it with his own hands. He tried to say "Humbug!" but stopped at the first syllable. Then, being much in need of rest, he went directly to bed and fell asleep.

| 4 |

The First of the Three Spirits

Scrooge awoke to the sound of a church bell counting out the time. To his great surprise, the heavy bell sounded 12 times. Then it stopped. It was past two when he went to bed. The clock was wrong. An icicle must have gotten into the works. *Twelve!*

"It isn't possible," said Scrooge, "that I can have slept through a whole day and far into another night." He got out of bed and went to the window. To see anything, he had to rub the frost off with the sleeve of his robe. All he could tell was that it was the middle of the night.

Scrooge went back to bed again and started to think. But the more he thought, the more perplexed he was. Had it all been a dream?

Marley's Ghost had upset him.

Scrooge lay in this state until the bells told

him it was 12:45. Then he remembered that the Ghost had warned him of a visit when the bell tolled one. The next 15 minutes passed slowly. Finally, the bell sounded, with a deep, dull, hollow, sad *one*. Light flashed in the room, and the curtains of the bed were drawn aside.

Scrooge found himself face to face with an unearthly visitor. It was a strange figure—like a child. Yet, it was not so much like a child as like an old man reduced to a child's size. Its hair was white with age, yet the face had not a wrinkle on it. It wore clothes of the purest white. Around its waist was a shining belt that sparkled and glittered. The visitor held a branch of fresh green holly in its hand. Its dress was trimmed with summer flowers. A bright clear glow came from the crown of its head, lighting the room.

"Are you the Spirit, sir, whose coming was foretold to me?" asked Scrooge.

"I am!" The voice was soft and gentle.

"Who—and what—*are* you?"

"I am the Ghost of Christmas Past."

"Long past?" asked Scrooge.

"No. Your past. I am here to save you."

Putting out its strong hand as it spoke, the Spirit clasped Scrooge gently by the arm.

"Rise, and walk with me!"

The grasp, though gentle, was not to be resisted. Scrooge rose. Then, seeing the Spirit moving toward the window, Scrooge said, "I am but a mortal! I will fall."

The Spirit laid its hand upon Scrooge's heart. Then he said, "Now you shall be upheld in more than this!" As the words were spoken, Scrooge and the Spirit passed through the wall. On the other side, they stood upon an open country road, bounded by fields. The city had vanished. The darkness and the mist had vanished with it. Now it was a clear, cold winter day. A blanket of snow was on the ground.

"Good heaven! Why, I was a boy here!" Scrooge cried.

The Spirit looked at him. Scrooge was aware of a thousand odors floating in the air. Each one was connected with a thousand thoughts, and hopes, and joys, and cares—all long, long forgotten!

"Your lip is trembling," said the Ghost. "And what is that upon your cheek?"

With a catch in his voice, Scrooge said it was a pimple. He begged the Ghost to lead him where he would.

"Do you remember the way?"

"Remember it?" cried Scrooge. "I could walk it blindfolded."

"Strange to have forgotten it for so many years!" said the Ghost. "Let us go on."

They walked along the road until they came to a little town. Some ponies came trotting toward them with boys upon their backs. These boys called to other boys in carts driven by farmers.

All the boys were in great spirits, laughing and shouting. The fields were so full of merry music that the crisp air laughed to hear it!

"These are but shadows of things that used to be," the Ghost explained to Scrooge. "They cannot see us."

As the boys rode by, Scrooge knew and named them, every one. Why was he so happy to see them? Why did his cold eye glisten and his heart leap as they went past? Why was he filled with gladness when he heard them say "Merry Christmas!" as they parted for their different homes? What was merry about Christmas to Scrooge? What good had it ever done him?

"The school is not quite deserted," said the Ghost. "One child, neglected by his friends, is left there still."

Scrooge said he knew it. And he sobbed.

They left the main road and went down a well-remembered lane. Soon they got to a mansion of dull red brick. It was a large house, but one of broken fortunes. The walls were damp and mossy. Many of the windows were broken, and the gates were decayed. Chickens clucked and strutted in the stables. The carriage houses and sheds were overrun with grass. The inside was just as run-down. The rooms were poorly furnished, cold, and vast. There was a harshness in the place. It spoke of too much getting up by candlelight, and too little to eat.

The Ghost led Scrooge across the hall to a room at the back of the house. It was a long, bare, sad room. A lonely boy was reading at a desk near a feeble fire. Scrooge sat down and wept to see the poor forgotten self of his boyhood.

The Spirit touched him on the arm and pointed to Scrooge's younger former self. Suddenly a man stood outside the window. He had an axe stuck in his belt and was leading a donkey laden with wood.

"Why, it's Ali Baba!" Scrooge exclaimed happily. "It's dear, old, honest Ali Baba! Yes, I remember! One Christmas when I was left here all alone, he came right out of the storybook to visit me! And look! There's the Sultan's Groom turned upside down by the Genie. Ha! I'm glad of it. He deserved it! What business had *he* to be married to the Princess!"

Scrooge's happy, excited face would have

been a surprising sight indeed to his business friends in the city.

"There's the Parrot!" cried Scrooge as he remembered yet another character from his books. For the only company Scrooge had in those days were the characters he read about. Then, feeling a stab of pity for his former self, he said, *"Poor boy!"*

"I wish..." Scrooge muttered, drying his eyes, "but it's too late now."

"What is the matter?" asked the Spirit.

"Nothing," said Scrooge. "There was a boy singing a carol at my door last night. I wish I had given him something, that's all."

The Ghost smiled thoughtfully. Then, waving its hand, it said, "Let us see another Christmas!"

| 5 |

Another
Christmas Past

As the Ghost and Scrooge looked on, Scrooge's former self grew older. The room became a little darker and dirtier. But there he was—alone again—when all the other boys had gone home for the jolly holidays.

Instead of reading, this time he was walking up and down in despair. Then the door opened. A little girl, much younger than the boy, ran in and put her arms about his neck. Kissing him, she called him her "dear, dear brother."

"I have come to bring you home, dear brother!" she said.

"Home, little Fan?" asked the boy.

"Yes!" said the girl, joyfully. "Home, for good and all. Home, for ever and ever. Father is so much kinder than he used to be. He sent me in a coach to bring you. And you are never to come back to this school again. But first, we'll have the merriest Christmas in all the world."

Scrooge turned to the Spirit and said, "She was always a delicate little thing. But she had a big heart!"

"She died a young woman," said the Ghost. "She had, I think, children."

"One child," said Scrooge.

"True," said the Ghost. "Your nephew!"

Feeling uneasy, Scrooge said, "Yes."

By now they had left the school behind them and were in a busy city. It was clear that it was Christmas time. It was evening, and the streets were lit up.

The Ghost stopped at a warehouse door, asking Scrooge if he knew the place.

"Know it!" cried Scrooge. "Why, I had my first job here!"

They went in the door. Upon seeing an old gentleman in a wig, Scrooge cried, "Why, it's old Fezziwig! Bless his heart. It's Fezziwig alive again!"

Old Fezziwig laid down his pen and looked up at the clock. It pointed to the hour of seven. He rubbed his hands, laughed, and called out in a rich, jolly voice: "Yo ho, there! Ebenezer! Dick!"

Scrooge's former self, now grown into a young man, came into the room. With him was his fellow apprentice.

"Dick Wilkins, to be sure!" said Scrooge to the Ghost. "Bless me, yes. There he is. He was very much attached to me, was Dick. Poor Dick! Dear, dear!"

"Yo ho, my boys!" said Fezziwig. "No more work tonight. It's Christmas Eve, Dick! Christmas, Ebenezer! Let's clear the floor and make lots of room here!"

In a minute, Dick and Ebenezer had cleared away every movable thing. The floor was swept, the lamps were trimmed, and coal was heaped upon the fire. The warehouse was soon as warm and dry and bright as any ballroom on Christmas Eve.

In came a fiddler, ready to play. In came Mrs. Fezziwig, one big substantial smile. In came the three Miss Fezziwigs, beaming and lovable. In came the six young men whose hearts they broke. In came all the young men and women working in the business. In came the housemaid, with her cousin, the baker. In

came the cook, the milkman, and the boy across the street. In they all came, one after another. The Fezziwigs made them all feel welcome, and everyone started dancing.

Finally old Fezziwig, clapping his hands to stop the music, cried out, "Well done!" At last the fiddler could take a break. But as soon as he had taken a drink, he began again. It was as if the old fiddler had been carried home, exhausted, and a new man had come to take his place at the fiddle.

There were more dances, and there was cake, and roast beef, and mince pies, and plenty to drink. At last old Fezziwig began to dance with Mrs. Fezziwig. As for her, she was worthy of being his partner in every sense of the term. If that's not high praise, tell me higher, and I'll use it.

When the clock struck 11, the party broke up. Mr. and Mrs. Fezziwig took their places, one on each side of the door. They shook hands with each person, wishing a Merry Christmas to all. Thus the cheerful voices died away, and the lads were left to their beds, which were in the back shop.

During all this time, Scrooge had acted like a man out of his wits. His heart and soul were in the scene—with his former self. He remembered everything, enjoyed everything, and was quite excited. It was not until now, when the bright faces of his former self and Dick had turned away, that he remembered the Ghost. He became aware that the Ghost was looking straight at him.

"A small matter," said the Ghost, "to make these silly folks so full of gratitude."

"Small?" echoed Scrooge.

The Spirit told Scrooge to listen to the two

apprentices talking. Dick and Ebenezer were pouring out their hearts in praise of Fezziwig. Then the Spirit said, "Why such praise? Fezziwig spent but a small amount of your mortal money. Is it so much that he deserves this praise?"

"It isn't that," said Scrooge. He seemed now to be speaking like his former, not his present, self. "It isn't that, Spirit. He has the power to make us happy or unhappy, to make our jobs light or heavy, a pleasure or a toil. You could say that his power lies in words and looks, in things you can't add or count up. But the happiness he gives is quite as great as if it had cost a fortune."

He felt the Spirit's glance, and stopped.

"What is the matter?" asked the Ghost.

"Nothing," said Scrooge.

"Something, I think?" the Ghost insisted.

"No," said Scrooge. "I should like to be able to say a word or two to my clerk just now. That's all."

"My time grows short," said the Spirit. "Quick!" Again, Scrooge saw himself. He was grown now, a man in the prime of life. His face had begun to wear the signs of care and greed. He was not alone this time, but sat by the side of a fair young girl. Tears were in her eyes.

"It matters little," she said, softly. "To you, very little. Another idol has replaced me. If it can cheer and comfort you in times to come, as I would have tried to do, I have no reason to be sad."

"What idol has replaced you?" he asked.

"Money," she said.

"This is the way of the world!" he said. "There is nothing so hard as poverty."

"You fear the world too much," she answered, gently. "All your other hopes have merged into the hope of avoiding poverty. That is all you care about."

"What, then? Perhaps I have grown that much wiser. My feelings toward you have not changed."

"Yes, they have. *You* are changed. You seem like another man. I now release you from your promise to marry me. I do this with a full heart—for love of the man you once were. You may feel pain over this. But in a brief time, you will get over it. May you be happy in the life you have chosen!"

She left him, and they parted.

"Spirit!" Scrooge cried out sadly. "Show me no more. Take me home now. Why do you torture me?"

"One more thing!" exclaimed the Ghost.

"No more!" cried Scrooge. "*No more*. I don't wish to see it!"

But the Ghost forced him to watch what happened next. They were in another scene and place. It was a room, not very large, but full of comfort. Next to the winter fire sat a beautiful young girl. She looked so much like the last one that Scrooge thought it was the same. Then he saw *her*—now a wife, sitting by her daughter. There was a lot of noise in the room, for there were more children there.

Then the father came home, carrying Christmas toys and presents. There were shouts of wonder and delight as each gift was received!

Finally, the father sat down at the fireside with his oldest daughter and her mother. "Belle," he said, turning to his wife with a smile. "I saw an old friend of yours this afternoon."

"Who was it?"

"Guess!"

"How can I? Oh, I know," she added in the same breath, laughing as he laughed. "Mr. Scrooge."

"Mr. Scrooge it was. I passed his office window. As it was not shut up, and he had a candle inside, I couldn't help seeing him. His partner lies upon the point of death, I hear. And there Scrooge sat alone. He's quite alone in the world, I do believe."

"Spirit!" said Scrooge in a broken voice. "Take me from this place. I cannot bear it!"

Suddenly Scrooge was overwhelmed with drowsiness. Then, finding himself in his own bed, he sank into a heavy sleep.

| 6 |

The Second of the Three Spirits

Scrooge awakened in the middle of a loud snore. He did not have to be told that it was almost 1:00. Pulling aside the bed curtains, he looked all around the bed. He did not wish to be taken by surprise.

Now, being ready for anything, he was not by any means ready for nothing. So, when the bell struck one, and no shape appeared, he began to tremble. Fifteen minutes went by, and still nothing came. All this time he lay on his bed, which was in a blaze of bright light. The light had been there since 1:00. Strangely, the light was more alarming than a dozen ghosts—for he did not know what it meant. At last, he began to think that the light might be coming from the next room. He got up and shuffled to the door in his slippers.

The moment Scrooge's hand was on the lock, a strange voice called him by name. It commanded him to enter, and he obeyed.

There was no doubt that it was Scrooge's own room. But it was decorated beautifully. The walls and ceiling were hung with living green, so it looked like a grove. From every part of it, bright berries glistened. The holly, mistletoe, and ivy reflected back the light, like so many mirrors. A mighty blaze roared up the chimney. Heaped on the floor—in a shape much like a throne—were piles of food. There were turkeys, geese, game, poultry, and strings of sausages. There were also pies, puddings, oysters, chestnuts, apples, oranges, pears, cakes, and bowls of punch. On this couch of food sat a jolly giant, glorious to see! He held a glowing torch up high. Its light shone down on Scrooge as he peeped around the door.

"Come in!" exclaimed the Ghost. "Come in, and know me better, man! I am the Ghost of Christmas Present. Look upon me!"

Scrooge did so. The Spirit wore a simple green robe, bordered with white fur. Its feet were bare. On its head it wore a holly wreath, set here and there with shining icicles. Its dark brown curls were long and free. It had a joyful look.

The Ghost of Christmas Present rose.

"Spirit," said Scrooge, "conduct me where you will. Last night, I learned a lesson that is working now. Tonight, if you have something to teach me, let me profit by it."

"Touch my robe!"

Scrooge did so. As he held it fast, all the food and decorations in the room vanished instantly. So did the room. Now they stood in the city streets on Christmas morning.

The people who were shoveling away the snow were joyful. They called out to one another now and then and threw a friendly snowball. The shops were still half open, and baskets of chestnuts tumbled out into the street. There were Spanish onions, and pears and apples piled high. There were bunches of grapes and piles of nuts begging to be carried home in paper bags and eaten after dinner.

There were heaps of raisins, almonds, and cinnamon sticks. Candied fruits, moist figs, and

French plums waited in their highly decorated boxes. Customers tumbled up against each other at the doors. Everyone seemed in the best mood possible.

Church bells then called the good people to the chapel. They flocked through the streets wearing their best clothes and happiest faces. All the while, the Spirit stood with Scrooge in a baker's doorway. As people passed, he sprinkled something from his torch on the dinners they carried. It was a very uncommon kind of torch. Once or twice, angry words were spoken by people who had bumped into each other. When the Spirit shed a few drops of water on them from the torch, their good humor was restored right away.

"Is there a special flavor in what you sprinkle from your torch?" asked Scrooge.

"There is. My own."

"Would it apply to any kind of dinner on this day?" asked Scrooge.

"Yes, but to a poor one most of all."

"Why to a poor one most?"

"Because it needs it most."

They went on, invisible as before, into the

suburbs of the town. Scrooge had noticed that the Ghost, in spite of his gigantic size, could fit in the smallest place with ease. Perhaps it was the pleasure the good Spirit had in showing off this power of his that led him straight to the home of Scrooge's clerk. Or perhaps it was his own kind, generous, hearty nature, and his sympathy with all poor men. In any case, there he went, and took Scrooge with him. Outside the door the Spirit smiled. Then he stopped to bless Bob Cratchit's dwelling with the sprinkling of his torch.

Mrs. Cratchit was setting the table with Belinda Cratchit, second of her daughters. Master Peter Cratchit plunged a fork into a big pot of potatoes. The two smaller Cratchits, boy and girl, came tearing in. They screamed that outside the baker's they had smelled a roasting goose—and had known it for their own. Thinking lovely thoughts about sage and onion, these young Cratchits danced about the table.

"Where is your precious father?" said Mrs. Cratchit. "And your brother, Tiny Tim! And Martha—she wasn't this late last year."

"Here's Martha, Mother!" said a girl, rushing in the door.

"Why, bless your heart, my dear. How late you are!" said Mrs. Cratchit.

"We had a lot of work to finish up last night," replied the girl. "And we couldn't leave until this morning, Mother!"

"Well, never mind, so long as you are here," said Mrs. Cratchit. "Sit down before the fire, my dear, and get warm."

"No, no! There's Father coming," cried the two young Cratchits. "Hide, Martha!"

So Martha hid herself, and in came Bob, the father, with Tiny Tim upon his shoulder. Alas for Tiny Tim. He carried a little crutch. His legs were supported by an iron frame!

"Why, where's our Martha?" cried Bob Cratchit, looking around.

"Not coming," said Mrs. Cratchit sadly.

"Not coming!" cried Bob. "Not coming on Christmas Day?"

Martha couldn't bear to see her father disappointed, even as a joke. So she popped out from behind the closet door and ran into his arms.

"And how did little Tim behave?" asked

Mrs. Cratchit.

"Why, as good as gold," said Bob, "and better!" As Tiny Tim sat by the fire, the rest of the family finished making the dinner. Mrs. Cratchit heated the gravy. Master Peter mashed the potatoes while Miss Belinda sweetened the applesauce. Martha dusted the hot plates. The two youngest Cratchits set chairs for everybody.

"There never was such a goose!" Bob said. Its tenderness and flavor, size and crisp skin, were all wonderful. After dinner, the pudding was brought out. Oh, a wonderful pudding! At last the dinner was all done, the table cleared, the hearth swept, and the fire made up. Then all the Cratchit family drew together around the hearth.

Bob served hot cider from a jug. The chestnuts on the fire sputtered and cracked noisily. Then Bob said, "A Merry Christmas to us all, my dears. God bless us!"

"God bless us every one!" said Tiny Tim.

"Spirit," said Scrooge, "Tiny Tim is sick. Tell me if he will live."

"I see a vacant seat," said the Ghost, "in the corner—and a crutch without an owner. If these shadows are unchanged by the future, the child will die."

"No, no!" cried Scrooge. "Oh, no, kind Spirit! Say he will be spared."

"If he is going to die, he had better do it, to decrease the surplus population."

Scrooge hung his head to hear his own words quoted by the Spirit. But, on hearing his own name, he looked up.

"Mr. Scrooge!" said Bob. "Let's drink to Mr. Scrooge, the Founder of the Feast!"

"The Founder of the Feast indeed!" cried Mrs. Cratchit. "I wish I had him here. I'd give him a piece of my mind."

"My dear," scolded Bob, "the children! It's Christmas Day."

"Only on Christmas Day would anyone drink to the health of such a stingy, hard, unfeeling man as Mr. Scrooge."

"My dear," was Bob's mild answer. "Remember—Christmas Day!"

"I'll drink to his health for *your* sake, Bob, but not for his. Long life to him!"

The children drank the toast after her. It was the first gloomy moment of the day. Scrooge was the ogre of the family. Just the mention of his name cast a dark shadow on the happy party.

But a few moments later, they were even merrier than before. They laughed and told stories about what they'd been doing lately.

By now it was getting dark and snowing heavily. As Scrooge and the Spirit went through the town, they saw how Christmas was being celebrated in every household. When they received the bright sprinklings of the Spirit's torch, the happy people became happier still.

| 7 |

More Christmas Presents

And now, without a word of warning from the Ghost, they stood upon a bleak moor. Huge stones were all around, as if it were the burial place of giants. Nothing grew there but moss and coarse grass.

"What place is this?" asked Scrooge.

"A place where miners live, those who work below the earth. They know me. See!"

A light shone from the window of a hut. Looking in, Scrooge and the Spirit saw a cheerful family dressed in holiday clothes. An old, old man and woman, with their children and their children's children and grandchildren, all gathered around a glowing fire. Led by the old man, they were singing Christmas songs.

The Spirit did not stay here. He told Scrooge to hold onto his robe, and they sped out to sea. To Scrooge's horror, looking back, he saw the last of the land disappear behind them. They soon came to a lonely lighthouse, some three miles from shore. Great heaps of seaweed clung to its base. Storm birds rose and fell about it.

But even here, two lighthouse tenders had made a fire. It shed a golden ray on the dark sea. Joining hands over their table, they wished each other Merry Christmas. The older one sang a Christmas song.

Again the Ghost sped on, high above the sea. Far from shore they saw a ship. They stood beside the helmsman at the wheel, the lookout in the bow, the officers on watch. Every man hummed a Christmas tune or had a Christmas thought. Every man had a kind word for another. Every man remembered those he cared for, and knew that they delighted to remember him.

It was a great surprise to Scrooge to hear a hearty laugh just then. It was an even greater surprise to find that the voice was his own nephew's. Now Scrooge was in a bright, dry, gleaming room. The Spirit stood, silent and smiling, by Scrooge's side.

"Ha, ha!" laughed Scrooge's nephew, merrily. "Ha, ha, ha!"

There is nothing in the world so contagious as laughter and good feeling. When Scrooge's nephew laughed, holding his sides and rolling his head, his wife laughed as merrily as he. Their friends roared with laughter, too.

"Ha, ha! Ha, ha, ha, ha!"

"He said that Christmas was a humbug, as sure as I live!" cried Scrooge's nephew. "He believed it, too!"

"More shame for him, Fred!" said his wife. She was a very pretty young woman. She had the sunniest pair of eyes you ever saw in anyone's head.

"He's a funny old fellow," said Scrooge's nephew. "That's the truth. And he certainly isn't as pleasant as he might be. However, I'm sure Uncle Scrooge's offenses carry their own punishment. It's not for me to say anything against him."

"I'm sure he is very rich, Fred," hinted his wife with a smile.

"What of that, my dear?" asked Scrooge's nephew. "His wealth is of no use to him.

He doesn't do any good with it. He doesn't make himself comfortable with it. Why, he doesn't even have the satisfaction of knowing he is going to help *us* with it!"

"Well, I have no patience for him," said his wife. All the other ladies quickly said the same thing.

"Oh, I have!" said Scrooge's nephew. "I am sorry for him. I couldn't be angry with him if I tried. Who suffers by his ill whims? *Himself*, always. Here, he takes it into his head to dislike us. He won't come and dine at our house. What's the result? He loses some pleasant moments—which certainly could do him no harm.

"I mean to give him the same chance every year, whether he likes it or not—for I *pity* him! He may rail at Christmas 'til he dies. But if I go there, in good temper, year after year, he can't help thinking better of it. Maybe he'd even think to leave his poor clerk 50 pounds. That would be something."

After tea, the friends enjoyed some music. As Scrooge listened, all the things that the Ghost of Christmas Past had shown him came to his mind. He thought that if he had listened to more music, years ago, he might be a happier man.

But they didn't spend the whole evening on music. After a while, there were games. They played blind man's bluff and then a game of How, When, and Where. Scrooge found himself joining in, even though nobody at the party could see him. The Ghost was very pleased to see Scrooge having so much fun. He begged like a boy to be allowed to stay until the guests left. But this the Spirit said could not be done.

"Here is a new game," said Scrooge. "Let me stay just one half-hour, Spirit!"

It was a game called Yes and No. Scrooge's nephew had to think of something, and the others had to guess what. They started to ask questions that could be answered yes or no. Soon the line of questioning revealed that Fred was thinking of an animal. It was a live animal, a disagreeable animal, a savage animal. It was an animal that growled and grunted sometimes, and talked sometimes, and lived in London. It walked about the streets. It wasn't led by anybody. It was not a horse, or a donkey, or a cow, or a bull. Nor was it a tiger, or a dog, or a pig, or a cat, or a bear.

At every question, Scrooge's nephew burst into a fresh roar of laughter. At last one guest, laughing loudly, cried out: "I know, Fred! I know what it is!"

"What is it?" cried Fred.

"It's your Uncle Scro-o-o-oge!"

Which it certainly was. Everyone laughed, but some objected that the answer to "Is it a bear?" should have been "Yes."

"Well, he has given us plenty of fun, I am sure," said Fred. "It would be ungrateful not to drink to his health. Here is a glass of hot cider. I say, 'To Uncle Scrooge!' "

"Well! Uncle Scrooge!" they cried.

"A Merry Christmas and a Happy New Year to the old man, whatever he is!" said Scrooge's nephew. "He wouldn't take it from me, but may he have it, nevertheless. Here's to Uncle Scrooge!"

Scrooge had become very light of heart. He might have thanked the company in a speech they couldn't hear. But the Ghost did not give him time. The whole scene passed away, and he and the Spirit were again upon their travels.

Much they saw, and far they went. Many homes they visited, and always with a happy end. The Spirit stood beside sick beds, and the people were cheerful. He stood on foreign lands, and they were close at home. He stood by struggling men, and they had hope. He stood by poverty, and it was rich. He left his blessing wherever he saw misery—and taught Scrooge his lessons.

It was a long night. It was strange, too, that while Scrooge stayed the same in appearance, the Ghost grew older. Looking at the Spirit, Scrooge noticed that its hair was turning gray.

"Are spirits' lives so short, then?" asked Scrooge.

"My life upon this globe is very brief," replied the Ghost. "It ends tonight."

"Tonight!" cried Scrooge in alarm.

"Tonight at midnight. Hark! The time is drawing near." The bells were ringing 11:45.

"Forgive me if I am rude in what I ask," said Scrooge. "But I see something strange coming from under your skirts. Is it a foot or a claw?"

"Look here," said the Spirit sadly.

From the folds of its robe came two small children. They were wretched, hideous, and miserable. Kneeling at the Spirit's feet, they clung to the outside of its robe.

They were a small boy and girl—yellow, ragged, scowling, wolfish, but also humble. Where graceful youth should have filled out their features, age had pinched and twisted them. Scrooge stared at them, horrified.

"Spirit! Whose children are these? Are they yours?" Scrooge could say no more.

"They are Humankind's," said the Spirit, looking down upon them. "And they cling to me. This boy is Ignorance. The girl is Want. Beware them both, and all like them. But most of all beware this boy. For on his brow I see Doom written, unless the writing be erased. Can you deny it?" cried the Spirit, stretching out its hand toward the city.

"Have they no refuge or hope?" cried Scrooge unhappily.

"Are there no prisons?" asked the Spirit, turning on Scrooge for the last time with his own words. *"Are there no workhouses?"*

The bell struck 12.

Scrooge looked about for the Ghost, and saw it not. As the last stroke faded, he remembered what Jacob Marley had said. Lifting his eyes, Scrooge saw a solemn Phantom, draped and hooded. It was coming, like a mist creeping along the ground, directly toward him.

| 8 |

The Third of the Three Spirits

The ghostly Phantom slowly and silently approached. It was covered in a deep black garment that left nothing visible but one outstretched hand. Except for this, it would have been difficult to separate the figure from the darkness around it.

"Am I in the presence of the Ghost of Christmas Yet to Come?" said Scrooge.

The Spirit answered not, but pointed ahead with its hand.

Although well used to ghostly company by this time, Scrooge feared this silent shape. His legs trembled beneath him. "Ghost of the Future!" he exclaimed. "I fear you more than any other spirit I have seen. But I know you are here to do me good. Because I hope to be another man from what I was, I will go with you. I do it with a thankful heart. Will you not speak to me?"

The Phantom gave him no reply. The hand was pointed straight before them.

"Lead on!" said Scrooge. "Lead on!"

The Phantom moved away as it had come toward him. Scrooge followed in the shadow of its flowing gown.

They scarcely seemed to enter the city. Rather, the city seemed to spring up about them. There they were, in the heart of it, among the merchants.

The Spirit stopped near one little knot of businessmen. Scrooge listened to their talk.

"I don't know much about it," said a fat man with a big chin. I only know he's dead."

"When did he die?" asked another.

"Last night, I believe."

"Why, what was the matter with him?" asked a third. "I thought he'd never die."

"God knows," said the first, yawning.

"What has he done with his money?"

"He hasn't left it to *me*—that's all I know!" The three men shared a laugh.

"It's likely to be a very cheap funeral," said the same speaker. "I don't know of anybody to go to it. Suppose we make up a party and volunteer?"

"I don't mind going—that is, if lunch is provided," said another. Another laugh.

The men strolled away and mixed with other groups. Scrooge knew the men. He looked toward the Spirit for an explanation.

The Phantom glided down the street. Its finger pointed to two persons who had stopped to talk. Scrooge knew these men also. They were men of business, very wealthy and important. Scrooge listened to what they were saying.

"Well!" said the first. "Old Scratch has got his own at last, hey?"

"So I hear. Cold, isn't it?"

"Just fine for Christmas time. Good morning!"

Not another word. Scrooge was at first surprised that the Spirit should listen in on such trivial conversations. Guessing there must be a hidden purpose, Scrooge thought about what it might be. It could not have anything to do with the death of Jacob, his former partner. That was Past—and this Ghost's only concern was the Future. He could not think of anyone to whom the conversations would apply.

Scrooge looked about for his own image, but another man stood in his usual place. Although the clock pointed to his usual time of day for being there, he saw no likeness of himself. Scrooge was not surprised, though. He had been thinking about changing his life. Perhaps this meant that he actually would!

Then the Phantom pointed ahead. They left the busy scene and went to a run-down area. Scrooge had never been there before. The shops and houses were wretched. The people were miserable and ugly.

In one dirty shop were piled heaps of rusty keys, nails, chains, files, scales, and bits of scrap iron. Sitting among these things, by a charcoal stove, was a gray-haired man, about 70 years of age.

As Scrooge and the Phantom came closer, a woman with a heavy bundle entered the shop. Then another woman and a man came in, each with similar bundles. They looked surprised to see one another. After a moment, all three burst into a loud laugh.

"Let the cleaning woman be first!" cried one woman. "Let the laundress be second, and let the undertaker's man be third. Look, Joe. See what we have."

"Come into the parlor," said the old man who was sitting by the stove. The parlor was the space behind a screen of ragged cloth. The first woman threw her bundle on the floor and sat on a stool. She looked boldly into the faces of the other two.

"What's wrong, then, Mrs. Dilber?" said the first woman. "Poor people have a right to take care of themselves. *He* always did."

"That's true! No man more so!" agreed the laundress.

"Very well, then!" cried the first woman. "Who's the worse for the loss of a few things like these? Not a dead man, I suppose?"

"No, indeed," said Mrs. Dilber, laughing.

"If he wanted to keep them after he was dead, why wasn't he natural in his lifetime? If he had been, somebody might have been there to look after him when Death came. Instead, he had to lie gasping out his last breath—alone by himself."

"The truest words that ever were said," agreed

Mrs. Dilber. "It serves him right."

"Open that bundle, old Joe, and tell me the value of it. Speak out plain. I'm not afraid to be the first—nor afraid for the others to see it. We knew that we were helping ourselves. It's no sin. Open the bundle, Joe."

But the man produced *his* bundle first. In it was a pencil case, a pair of sleeve buttons, and a pin of no great value. Joe added up the value and said, "Who's next?"

Mrs. Dilber was next. There were sheets, a few towels, some clothes, two small silver teaspoons, and a few boots. Joe added up the value in the same way.

"Now undo *my* bundle, Joe," said the first woman.

Joe untied a great many knots, and then dragged out a large and heavy roll of some dark stuff. "What do you call this?" said Joe. "Is it bed curtains?"

"Ah!" said the woman, laughing. "Bed curtains!"

"You don't mean to say you took them down with him lying there?" asked Joe.

"Yes, I do," said the woman. "Why not?

I won't hold my hand back when I can get something in it by reaching out. Think about the kind of man he was, anyway! Don't drop that lamp oil on the blankets, now."

"*His* blankets?" asked Joe.

"Whose do you think? He isn't likely to get cold without them, I dare say."

"Well, I hope he didn't die of anything catching, eh?" said old Joe.

"Don't you be afraid of that," said the woman. "You may look through that shirt 'til your eyes ache, but you won't find a hole in it. It's the best he had, and a fine one, too. They'd have wasted it, if not for me."

"What do you call *wasting* it?" asked old Joe with a sly look.

"Putting it on him to be buried in, to be sure," replied the woman with a laugh. "Somebody was fool enough to do it, but I took it off again. Cheap calico is just as good for the purpose. He can't look uglier than he did in that one."

Scrooge listened to this talk in horror. He viewed the people with hate and disgust.

"Ha! Ha!" laughed the same woman, when Joe paid them. "This is the end of it, you see! He frightened everyone away from him when he was alive. He didn't know he would profit *us* when he was dead! Ha, ha, ha!"

"Spirit!" said Scrooge, shuddering. "I see, I see. The case of this unhappy man might be my own. My life tends that way, now. But look! Good heaven, what is *this*?"

| 9 |

A Christmas Future?

The scene had suddenly changed. Now Scrooge stood beside a bed. It was a bare bed with no curtains. Beneath a thin sheet there lay a body, covered up from head to toe.

The room was dark, except for a pale light coming in from outside. This light fell straight upon the covered figure. Lying there, unwatched, unwept, uncared for, was the body of a dead man.

Scrooge looked at the Phantom. Its hand was pointing to the head. One motion of Scrooge's finger would have lifted the cover and revealed the face. Scrooge thought of it, knowing how easy it would be to do. He longed to lift the sheet, but he seemed to have no power to do so.

Scrooge wondered—if this man could be brought back to life now, what would be his thoughts? The dead man lay in the dark, empty house, with not a man, woman, or child to say a kind word about him. A cat was tearing at the door. The sound of gnawing rats could be heard beneath the fireplace. What rats wanted in the room of death, Scrooge did not dare to think.

"Spirit!" he said. "This is a fearful place. In leaving it, I shall not leave its lesson—trust me. Let us go!"

Still the Ghost pointed with an unmoved finger to the dead man's head.

"I understand you," Scrooge said, "and I would do it if I could. But I have not the power, Spirit. I have not the power."

Again it seemed to look upon him.

"Is there any person in the town who feels emotion caused by this man's death?" asked Scrooge. "If so, show that person to me, I beg you!"

For a moment, the Phantom spread its dark robe out to the side like a wing. Then, as it lowered its arm and the sleeve fell away, a room was revealed. A young mother and her small children were there.

The woman seemed to be expecting someone—for she walked up and down the room impatiently. She started at every sound. She looked out the window, glanced at the clock, and tried to sew.

At last, a knock was heard. The woman hurried to the door and met her husband. Although his face was very young, it was sad and worn with care.

The man sat down to the dinner that had been waiting for him. When the wife asked about the news, he seemed too embarrassed and uneasy to answer.

"Is it good?" she said. "Or bad?"

"Bad," he answered.

"We are quite ruined?"

"No. There is hope yet, Caroline."

"If only he gives in," she said, "there is! Nothing is past hope—if such a miracle has happened!"

"He is past giving in," said her husband. "He is dead."

She was a good woman, but she was thankful in her soul to hear it. Clasping her hands, she said so. The next moment, she prayed for forgiveness and was sorry. But the first emotion spoke the truth in her heart.

"To whom will our debt be transferred?"

"I don't know. But before that time we shall be ready with the money. We may sleep tonight with light hearts, Caroline!"

Yes, their hearts did grow lighter. The children's faces were brighter. It was a happier house for this man's death! It seemed the only emotion the Ghost could show Scrooge was one of pleasure.

"Let me see someone who is *sorry* about the death. Otherwise, Spirit, that dark chamber will be forever present to me."

Next the Ghost brought Scrooge to poor Bob Cratchit's house. They found the mother and the children seated around the fire.

It was quiet. Very quiet. The noisy little Cratchits were as still as statues in one corner. The mother laid her sewing upon the table, and put her hand up to her face.

"The color hurts my eyes," she said. "But for all the world I wouldn't show weak eyes to your father when he comes home. It must be near his time."

"*Past* it rather," Peter answered. "But I think he has walked a little slower than he used to these few last evenings, Mother."

They were quiet again. At last she said, "He used to walk very fast indeed, with—with Tiny Tim upon his shoulder. But the little fellow was very light to carry. And your father loved him so, it was no trouble. *No* trouble! Ah, there is your father at the door!"

She hurried out to meet him. His tea was ready for him, and they all tried to serve it to him first. Then the two young Cratchits climbed on his knees and said, "Don't mind it, Father. Don't be sad!"

"I went to the cemetery today, my dears," said Bob. "I wish you could have gone. It would have done you good to see how green a place it is. But you'll see it often. I promised Tim that I would walk there on Sundays. My poor little child!" he cried. "My dear child!"

He broke down all at once. He couldn't help it. When he composed himself, he said, "I am sure that none of us shall ever forget our dear Tiny Tim—shall we?—or this first parting there was among us?"

"*Never*, Father!" they all cried.

"Spirit," said Scrooge. "Our parting moment is at hand. I am sad about Tiny Tim's death. But tell me who that man was we saw lying dead?"

The Ghost of Christmas Yet to Come pointed straight ahead. They began to move forward. As they passed his own office, Scrooge looked in. It was an office still, but not *his*. The furniture was not the same, and the figure in the chair was not himself. The Phantom pointed as before.

Moving on again they soon reached an iron gate. Scrooge looked around before entering.

A churchyard. Here, then, the wretched man whose name he had now to learn, lay underneath the ground. The Spirit stood among the graves, and pointed down to one. Scrooge went toward it, trembling.

"Before I go on," said Scrooge, "answer just one question. Are these the shadows of the things that will be, or of the things that only *may* be?"

Still the Ghost pointed to the grave.

Scrooge crept toward it, trembling as he went. Following the finger, he read his own

name upon the stone of the neglected grave: EBENEZER SCROOGE.

"Am *I* that man who lay upon the bed?" Scrooge cried, falling to his knees.

The finger pointed from the grave to Scrooge, and back again.

"No, Spirit! Oh, *no, no!*"

Still the finger pointed.

"Spirit!" Scrooge cried. "Hear me! I am not the man I was. I will not be the man I would have been but for these visits. Why show me this, if I am past all hope?"

71

For the first time the hand appeared to shake a little.

"Good Spirit, I can see that you have pity on me. Tell me that I may yet change these shadows you have shown me. *Tell me I can change my life!*"

The uplifted hand trembled.

"I will honor Christmas in my heart, and try to keep it all the year," Scrooge cried out. "I will live in the Past, the Present, and the Future. The Spirits of all Three shall strive within me. From now on I will not shut out the lessons they teach. Oh, tell me that I may wash away the writing on this stone!"

In his agony, Scrooge caught the Spirit's hand. It tried to free itself, but Scrooge was strong. At last the Spirit, stronger yet, freed its hand and pulled it away.

Reaching up in a last prayer to change his fate, Scrooge saw the Phantom's hood and gown begin to flutter. In a moment it collapsed, dwindling down into a bedpost.

| **10** |

The End of It

Yes! And the bedpost was his own. The bed was his own, the room was his own. Best of all—the time before him was his own.

"I will live in the Past, the Present, and the Future!" Scrooge repeated as he jumped out of bed. His face was wet with grateful tears.

"They are not torn down," cried Scrooge, touching his bed curtains. "They are here! I am here! The things that would have been, may yet be changed. They *will* be!"

Now Scrooge was laughing and crying in the same breath. "I don't know what to do! I am as light as a feather. I am as happy as an angel. I am as merry as a schoolboy. A merry Christmas to everybody! A happy New Year to all the world!"

Really, for a man who had been out of practice for so many years, Scrooge's laugh was wonderful. Perhaps it was the father of a long, long line of brilliant laughs!

Running to the window, he opened it and put out his head. No fog, no mist. Bright, happy cold. Golden sunlight. Heavenly sky. Sweet fresh air. Merry bells. Oh, glorious! *Glorious!* "What's today?" cried Scrooge, waving his arm at a boy in the street.

"Why, it's Christmas Day," said the boy.

"Christmas Day!" Scrooge exclaimed to himself. "I haven't missed it! The Spirits have done it all in one night. They can do anything they like. Of course they can." Then, to the boy, he said, "Do you know the poultry shop at the corner?"

"I should hope so," replied the lad.

"An intelligent boy!" said Scrooge. "A remarkable boy! Do you know if they've sold the prize turkey that was hanging in the window? Not the little one—the big one?"

"What, the one as big as me?"

"What a delightful boy!" said Scrooge. "Yes, lad! The big one!"

"It's hanging there now," said the boy.

"Is it?" said Scrooge. "Go and buy it. Come back with the man, and I'll give you a shilling.

Come back in less than five minutes, and I'll give you half a crown!"

The boy was off like a shot.

"I'll send the turkey to Bob Cratchit's!" whispered Scrooge. He rubbed his hands, laughing. "He won't know who sent it. Why, that bird is twice the size of Tiny Tim!"

Scrooge quickly wrote the address and went downstairs to open the door and wait for the poultry man. As he stood there, the door knocker caught his eye. "I shall love it as long as I live!" cried Scrooge, patting it with his hand. "It's a wonderful knocker! Here's the turkey! Hello! Merry Christmas!"

And what a turkey! It never could have stood upon its legs, that bird, it was so fat!

"Why, you can't *carry* that, boy!" said Scrooge. "You must have a cab."

He chuckled as he said this. He chuckled as he paid for the turkey and for the cab. And he chuckled when he paid the boy. Then he chuckled when he sat down in his chair. He went on chuckling until he cried.

He dressed himself "all in his best," and went out into the streets. By this time many people were pouring forth, just as he had seen them with the Ghost of Christmas Present. Walking with his hands behind him, Scrooge greeted each face with a delighted smile. He looked so pleasant that three amazed-looking men sputtered, "Good morning, sir! A Merry Christmas to you!"

He had not gone far when he saw one of the men who had come to his office the day before. Now he hurried up to him and said, "How do you do? I hope you did well in your collections yesterday. It was very kind of you. A Merry Christmas to you, sir!"

"Mr. Scrooge?" the man gasped.

"Yes," said Scrooge. "That is my name, although I fear it may not be pleasant to you. Allow me to ask your pardon. And would you kindly have the goodness to accept—" Here Scrooge whispered in his ear.

"Lord bless me!" cried the gentleman. "My dear Mr. Scrooge, are you serious?"

"Oh, a great many back payments are included in that amount, I assure you."

"My dear sir!" the man cried. "I don't know how to thank you."

"Don't say another word, please," said Scrooge. "Come and see me, will you?"

"I *will*!" cried the beaming gentleman.

"Thank you," said Scrooge. "I thank you 50 times. Bless you!"

Scrooge went to church and then walked about the streets. He watched the happy faces of the people and patted children on the head. In the afternoon, he headed toward his nephew's house.

He passed the door a dozen times before he had the courage to go up and knock. Finally, he did it. When he was let in, he marched toward the dining room and opened the door. "Fred!"

he called out.

"Why, bless my soul!" Fred cried in amazement. "Who's that?"

"It's I—your Uncle Scrooge. I have come to dinner. Will you still welcome me, Fred?"

Welcome? It was a wonder Fred didn't shake his arm off! Scrooge was made to feel at home in five minutes. Wonderful party, wonderful games, wonderful happiness!

The next morning, Scrooge went to the office early. If he could only be there first, and catch Bob Cratchit coming late! That was the thing he had his heart set upon.

And he did it. Yes, he did! Bob came hurrying in a full 18 minutes late.

"Hello!" growled Scrooge, in his old voice, as near as he could pretend it. "What do you mean by coming in late?"

"I am very sorry, sir," said Bob. "It's only once a year, sir. It shall not be repeated. I was making rather merry yesterday, sir."

"Now, I'll tell you what, my friend," said Scrooge. "I am not going to stand for this sort of thing any longer. And therefore. . . *I am about to raise your salary!* A Merry

Christmas, Bob! I'll raise your salary, and try to help your struggling family. We will discuss it this very afternoon, over a cup of Christmas punch. Make up the fires now. And buy some more coal before you dot another i, Bob Cratchit!"

Scrooge was better than his word. He did all that he had promised, and much more. To Tiny Tim, who did *not* die, he became a second father. As time went on, Scrooge became as good a man as the good old city ever knew. Some people laughed to see such a change in him—and he let them laugh. Scrooge's own heart could now laugh, too—and that was quite enough for him.

Scrooge had no more meetings with the Spirits. But it was always said of him that he knew how to keep Christmas well—if any man alive ever could. May that be truly said of all of us! And so, as Tiny Tim observed, God bless us, every one!

Activities
A Christmas Carol

BOOK SEQUENCE
Number the events to show which happened first, second, and so on.

_____ 1. Scrooge checked to see that nobody was in the closet.

_____ 2. Bob promised to be in the office early the next morning.

_____ 3. After dinner, Mrs. Cratchit brought out the Christmas pudding.

_____ 4. Scrooge said that Marley was always a good man of business.

_____ 5. Scrooge asked Fred why he got married.

_____ 6. The Ghost of Christmas Present was a jolly giant in a fur-trimmed green robe.

_____ 7. Scrooge said he helped to support workhouses and prison.

_____ 8. The Ghost of Christmas Past looked like a child-sized old man.

_____ 9. Scrooge promised to remember the lessons taught by the Spirits.

_____ 10. The Ghost of Christmas Yet to Come wore a hooded black gown.

_____ 11. To chase the caroler away, Scrooge struck the door with a ruler.

FACTS ABOUT CHARACTERS

Circle the sentences that describe each character.

1. **Jacob Marley**

   a. Marley was not liked and would not be missed.

   b. Everyone who knew Marley felt sorrow for his death.

2. **Scrooge**

   a. He enjoyed celebrating Christmas and helping the poor.

   b. He thought celebrating anything was too foolish, especially celebrating Christmas.

3. **Bob Cratchit**

   a. He was a kind hearted but poorly paid clerk in Scrooge's office.

   b. He was a poorly paid clerk in Scrooge's office so he hated him.

4. **The ghosts of Christmas**

   a. They wanted to punish Scrooge for his berating Christmas.

   b. They wanted to help Scrooge get back his early kindness and warm heart.

5. **Fred**

   a. Fred was Scrooge's good natured nephew.

   b. Even though Fred was a son of Scrooge's deceased sister, he didn't like Scrooge.

6. **Fezziwig**

   a. Fezziwig was Scrooge's severe and harsh former employer.

   b. Fezziwig was Scrooge's kind and generous former employer.

7. **Belle**

   a. She was Scrooge's wife.

   b. She was Scrooge's long-ago sweetheart.

TRUE OR FALSE

Write **T** or **F** to show whether each statement below is *true* or *false*.

1. ___ When Jacob Marley died, Scrooge was Marley's only mourner.

2. ___ When two gentleman visit Scrooge's office asking for donations for the poor, Scrooge rants and raves in response, giving them nothing.

3. ___ Scrooge was surprised to see the face of Christmas Spirit on the door knocker.

4. ___ Scrooge and the Ghost of Christmas Past visited the school where young Ebenezer happily celebrated holidays with other students.

5. ___ When Scrooge worked as a clerk at Fezziwig's warehouse, he was really happy at the Christmas party.

6. ___ In spite of the Cratchits' modest circumstances and ill health of their youngest child, Tiny Tim, they enjoyed a good deal of happiness.

7. ___ Scrooge and the Ghost of Christmas Present visited Fred's house. They saw his nephew ask the guests to join him in a toast to Scrooge's health.

8. ___ The Ghost of Christmas Yet to Come shows Scrooge three gentlemen talking about an unnamed man who has died, showing little sympathy or sense of loss.

9. ___ When Scrooge saw his name on a tombstone in the churchyard, he begged to for another chance to "wash away the writing on the stone."

10. ___ Awakening in his own room, Scrooge was joyous because he could resolve to rewrite the future he had been shown.

COMPREHENSION CHECK
Reread Chapter 3 and answer below.

A. Write a letter to show how each sentence should be completed.

1. ___ As he turned the key in the lock, Scrooge saw

2. ___ Scrooge liked darkness because

3. ___ Scrooge heard a clanking noise below that

4. ___ A living person must walk among his fellows or

5. ___ Marley said that Scrooge still had a chance to

6. ___ Marley said his real business on earth was

a. do so in death.

b. escape the same fate.

c. sounded like heavy chains dragging.

d. Marley's face looking at him.

e. charity, mercy, and kindness.

f. it was cheap.

B. Complete the sentences using the words from the box.

| pigtail | padlocks | witness | spirits |

1. Marley's hair was done up in a _____.

84

2. Marley's chain was made of ledgers, cash boxes, and _____.

3. Marley's fate was to _____ what he had not shared on earth.

4. Marley tells Scrooge that three _____ will come to haunt him.

INFERENCE

Reread Chapter 7. Then circle a letter to show how each sentence should be completed.

1. Scrooge saw Christmas being celebrated in a humble miner's hut and in a lonely lighthouse. By taking Scrooge there, what point was the Spirit making?

   a. that Christmas isn't happy for poor people

   b. that Christmas spirit doesn't depend on money

2. What did Fred mean when he said that Scrooge's "offenses carry their own punishment"?

   a. Meanness to others hurts the mean person most.

   b. Scrooge should sentence himself to a prison term.

3. Why does Fred say he is sorry for his uncle?

   a. because he has no loving wife or children

   b. because he misses out on many good times

4. Why did Scrooge beg the Spirit to let him stay at Fred's until the party was over?

   a. Scrooge wanted to hear what they said about him.

   b. Scrooge was enjoying the music and the games.

5. Why did Fred insist that his guests "drink to Scrooge's health?"

   a. Scrooge had given them a lot of laughs.

   b. Scrooge was old and in poor health.

6. Two ragged scowling children appeared from the folds of the Spirits' robe. What did these children represent?

   a. all the children of the world who suffer from poverty and lack of education

   a. the kind of tiresome people who should be sent to prisons and workhouses

FINAL EXAM
Circle a letter to answer the question or correctly complete each statement.

1. On what day did Marley die seven years ago?

   a. on Christmas day

   b. on New Year's Eve

   c. on Christmas Eve

   d. on a Sunday night

2. Before leaving the office, Bob's last task was to

   a. turn off the air conditioner.

   b. sweep the floor.

   c. fill in his timesheet.

   d. snuff out the candle.

3. Both Scrooge and his suite of rooms were
   a. old, dreary, and chilly.
   b. smart, stylish and new
   c. smelly and filthy.
   d. warm and inviting.

4. What did Marley regret most about his life?
   a. that he hadn't earned enough money
   b. that Scrooge had been his partner
   c. that he had been blind to the needs of others
   d. that he hadn't taken better vacations

5. How was Scrooge's nephew like Fan, his mother?
   a. Both lived to a ripe old age.
   b. Both were interested in Scrooge's money.
   c. Both were abused by Scrooge.
   d. Both were kind and loving to Scrooge.

6. Throughout the story the Cratchits represent
   a. families who live well in spite of hardships.
   b. people who are too lazy to get better jobs.
   c. people with little hope or confidence.
   d. sad families who pretend to be happy.

7. What sad event would happen if the future didn't change?
   a. Bob Cratchit would lose his job.
   b. Christmas would be canceled.
   c. Tiny Tim would soon die.
   d. Scrooge would become young again.

Answers to Activities
A Christmas Carol

BOOK SEQUENCE
1. 5   2. 4   3. 10   4. 6   5. 1   6. 8
7. 2   8. 7   9. 11   10. 9   11. 3

FACTS ABOUT CHARACTERS
1. a   2. b   3. a   4. b   5. a   6. b   7. b

TRUE OR FALSE
1. T   2. T   3. F   4. F   5. T   6. T
7. F   8. F   9. T   10. T

COMPREHENSION CHECK
A. 1. d   2. f   3. c   4. a   5. b   6. e
B. 1. pigtail   2. padlocks   3. witness   4. spirits

INFERENCE
1. b   2. a   3. b   4. b   5. a   6. a

FINAL EXAM: 1. c   2. d   3. a   4. c   5. d   6. a   7. c